HORSE DIARIES
· Lily ·

to Delila

from Mack

HORSE DIARIES

Lily

WHITNEY SANDERSON

illustrated by RUTH SANDERSON

RANDOM HOUSE 🏠 NEW YORK

Text copyright © 2018 by Whitney Robinson
Cover art and interior illustrations copyright © 2018 by Ruth Sanderson
Photograph credits: © Bob Langrish (p. 141); © Mary Evans Picture Library (p. 143)

Visit us on the Web! rhcbooks.com

Educators and librarians, for a variety of teaching tools, visit us at
RHTeachersLibrarians.com

Library of Congress Cataloging-in-Publication Data
Names: Sanderson, Whitney, author. | Sanderson, Ruth, illustrator.
Title: Lily / Whitney Sanderson ; illustrated by Ruth Sanderson.
Description: First Edition. | New York : Random House, [2018] | Series: Horse diaries ; #15 |
Summary: In 1939 Wales, a strawberry roan Welsh pony named Lily and her rider Gwen
are Pony Club members who enjoy competing in gymkhana games, but the start of
World War II brings changes to their routine and a new member to the Pony Club—a prickly
girl named Bridget, sent to the country to escape the threat of bombings in London.
Identifiers: LCCN 2017012209 | ISBN 978-1-5247-6654-2 (paperback) |
ISBN 978-1-5247-6655-9 (lib. bdg.) | ISBN 978-1-5247-6656-6 (ebook)
Subjects: LCSH: Welsh pony—Juvenile fiction. | CYAC: Welsh pony—Fiction. |
Ponies—Fiction. | Pony Club games—Fiction. | Friendship—Fiction. | World War,
1939-1945—Wales—Fiction. | Wales—History—20th century—Fiction. | BISAC:
JUVENILE FICTION / Animals / Horses. | JUVENILE FICTION / Holidays &
Celebrations / Easter & Lent. | JUVENILE FICTION / Sports & Recreation / Equestrian.
Classification: LCC PZ10.3.S217 Li 2018 | DDC [Fic]—dc23

Printed in the United States of America
10 9 8 7 6 5 4 3 2 1
First Edition

Random House Children's Books supports the First Amendment
and celebrates the right to read.

My special thanks to
Ursula Roberts and Charlotte Rowell
for sharing their Pony Club knowledge

—W.S.

For Diane and her team of young riders at
Heritage Farm in Easthampton, Massachusetts

—R.S.

CONTENTS

"Oh! if people knew what a comfort to horses a light hand is . . ."
—from *Black Beauty*, by Anna Sewell

HORSE DIARIES
· Lily ·

Gymkhana
Great Britain, 1939

Bang! The cork gun fired in the air, and I leaped forward into a gallop. The noise had spooked me, but I didn't break stride. Apricot's bright eye gleamed beside mine, keeping pace with me. Not far behind, I heard the rhythmic snorting of the cob mare from the South Notts team.

At our home meets in Carmarthenshire, the starter always dropped a flag to begin a race. But today we were guests of the Eridge Hunt Pony Club, over the border in Sussex, England. This was fox-hunting country, and the ponies here were used to the sound of a gunshot.

I focused ahead, to the wooden buckets standing in a row at the end of the roped-off meadow. My ten-year-old rider, Gwen, slowed me as we drew near. She kicked her feet out of the stirrups and slid down from my back before I had fully halted.

"Whoa, Lily, stand," she said. I was riled from the race, so I couldn't help pawing the grass a little. But I didn't *really* move from the spot.

Holding my reins in one hand, Gwen kneeled

in front of a bucket brimming with water and apples. She plunged her face into the water. I couldn't help wishing it were the ponies, not the riders, who competed in this part of the game. I'd have gotten two or three apples by now!

Apricot's rider, Susan Padmore, was bobbing for an apple, too. I wished Gwen would hurry up. Apricot was my rival on the Eridge Hunt team. She was a fine-boned chestnut mare who looked, and ran, like a miniature Thoroughbred. She had won the Pony Jumper championship at the summer rally. Now I was eager to even the score.

At last Gwen lifted her dripping face from the bucket. She had an apple clenched in her teeth. A moment later Susan bit into an apple, too. Almost at the same time, the two girls mounted and galloped us back across the meadow.

Apricot and I were neck and neck again. We could have been hitched in the same harness. I strained to lengthen my stride. Inch by inch, I managed to pull ahead—and nearly crashed into my teammate's rump as we crossed the finish line.

Good show, Lily! You looked ready to race in the Epsom Oaks. Cadfael, a bright bay Welsh

Mountain pony, reached out and gave me a friendly nip on the flank.

"Stop being a beast, Caddy!" His rider, Gwen's best friend, Rhiannon Kiffin, tugged his reins to turn his head away from me. But Cadfael wasn't being mean. It was just his nature to nibble on everything. Nearby, fussy Arian laid back his ears.

He wore the red ribbon of a kicker in his tail, so everyone knew not to pass too close behind him.

Gwen dropped her apple into a bucket near the finish line. The next pair, Catrin Pritchard and Seren, took off. Like me, Seren was a registered Welsh pony. His name meant "star," and his palomino coat gleamed like the golden horse atop a trophy. We even had the same great-grandsire, Dyoll Starlight.

Seren stood like a rock while Catrin splashed around for an apple, then galloped hard on the homestretch. They finished with a few lengths' lead over the other teams.

Rhiannon was next. She gave Cadfael a big kick as they bolted across the chalk line in the grass.

"Quiet aids!" called Rowena, our instructor.

She had driven us here early this morning in her green truck and rust-colored trailer. All day she kept her hawk-sharp eye on the team to ensure that everyone was riding safely and showing proper Pony Club spirit. That meant our riders must help out anyone who needed it and not be sore losers or gloating winners. It also meant that we ponies mustn't lay back our ears or make faces at the other teams' mounts to intimidate them.

Cadfael and Rhiannon set a blazing pace. But Cadfael was overexcited and didn't stop when he reached the buckets. He kept galloping across the meadow. When Rhiannon finally got him turned around, he trampled in circles around the bucket, and I was afraid he'd knock it over. That would disqualify our team!

But Rhiannon bit into her apple quickest of

all. Carmarthenshire still had a small lead by the time Cadfael flashed across the finish line.

Unfortunately, the last pair was little Nan Hughes on Arthur.

Each race had four laps, and our Pony Club had nine members. It was only fair that even the youngest and newest riders got to have a turn. But to send Arthur out for the anchor lap? It seemed a poor strategy. He was so wide, and seven-year-old Nan's legs were so short, that her kicks only managed to coax him into a reluctant trot.

"Your stick, Nan, use your stick!" hollered Gwen. Nan didn't like to use her riding crop, but it was the only tool with the power to make Arthur canter. Now she lifted her arm and gave the pony a firm swat on the flank. Arthur broke into a reluctant canter.

Nan had trouble biting into the slippery, wet apples, but eventually she got one. We ponies stamped and whinnied to Arthur as he lumbered down the homestretch.

Look sharp, Arthur, stout lad! nickered Seren.

For Pony Club, for glory! called Huw.

Churn those hooves, Old Blossom. . . .

It was only this last cry from Cadfael that urged Arthur into a true gallop. You see, Arthur had a piebald color that, combined with his large girth, made him bear a striking resemblance to a black-and-white milk cow.

Cadfael's nickname was the only thing I had known to annoy good-natured Arthur. As a result, he thundered toward the finish line with a speed that would be unremarkable to most onlookers but was astonishing to those who knew him. It was enough. Arthur's spotted nose crossed the finish line a whisker ahead of Eridge Hunt's pony.

The riders cheered for Nan. Her round face blushed to the tips of her ears. Arthur arched his neck with pride and looked almost regal.

But I was distracted from his moment of glory by the pail of apples near the finish line. The fact that they were bitten and bruised only made them smell sweeter. Gwen didn't notice the reins sliding through her fingers. . . .

"I'd better not see anyone letting their ponies eat apples with bits in their mouths!" called Rowena. Gwen noticed me nosing toward the bucket and led me a little ways off.

"I'll give you one later, Lily," she said, patting my neck.

Then she made a face and ran a finger around the inside of her high collar. I could tell she hated the stiff show clothes that the Pony Clubbers wore to rallies—flared buff jodhpurs, a black velvet-covered helmet, and shiny knee-high leather boots. This was her first pair of tall boots, instead of the ankle-high boots that younger children wore. Her outfit was completed by the blue-and-gold Pony Club pin gleaming on the lapel of her show jacket.

We had hardly a moment to catch our breath

before Rowena announced the riders for the next race: Glenn Kiffin and Eryl, Winnifred Kiffin and Taffy, Dylan Kiffin and Huw, and Luc Thomas and Arian. Megan Kiffin pouted at that, for she had only run in two races. Rowena promised her a spot in the next race, the last of the day.

You might have noticed a great many Kiffins in the Pony Club. At fifteen, Winnifred was the eldest, followed by Megan and Glenn, the twelve-year-old twins. Rhiannon was ten years old, like Gwen, and Dylan had just joined Pony Club this year, at six.

With so many mouths to feed, the Kiffins had bought all their ponies at bargain prices from auctions. Cadfael's old owners had given him away after his young rider broke her arm being bucked off him. Taffy was a pretty jumper but prone to running out in front of fences. There was also Snowdrop, Megan's shaggy cob gelding, and Eryl, who was what horse folk called a "hard keeper," always a bit skinny and often sick or lame. Finally there was Huw, a bay pony so old that his joints creaked when he walked.

The club's non-Kiffin members were Nan and Arthur, Catrin and Seren, and thirteen-year-old Luc Thomas and Arian, who were both fierce and handsome and a bit arrogant.

The Carmarthenshire Pony Club was a bit of a ragtag crew compared with the perfectly turned out ponies of the Eridge Hunt and South Notts teams. Cadfael, in particular, looked a bit shabby with his knobby braids sticking up in all directions—Rhiannon never had the patience to do them properly. But Rowena often reminded us that how our team performed was more important than how we looked. And we were ready to race!

In the next event, the sack relay, the teams would gallop once more to the end of the meadow. The riders would dismount and pull a burlap feed sack over their legs. Then they would hop back to the finish line—like darling bunny rabbits— leading their ponies beside them.

Right away, it became clear that this would not be our club's finest hour.

Huw did his best, but his canter was slower than most ponies' trots. Taffy decided she was spooked by the pile of sacks and wouldn't even get near them.

Eryl often got shin splints, so she wore snowy-white polo wraps to protect her legs. She cantered with an unusually high-stepping gait to show them off, which set us even farther behind.

Luc was too busy arguing with Rowena that the sack race was "stupid" to notice that his turn had come. When he finally set off, he refused to hop properly in his sack. He just sort of shuffled with a scowl on his face. Arian seemed embarrassed, too, and minced along with his ears back.

We finished dead last in the race.

I thought of the red first-prize rosettes that the winning team would receive. When I won red rosettes, Gwen hung them on my stall door.

"Gwen and Lily, you'll run anchor for the last race," said Rowena. My ears perked up at the sound of my name.

Then the announcer called out the standings over the loudspeaker, surprising us all.

"Our three teams are tied now, with twenty-seven points each," said the magnified voice. "It's a dead heat, as they say on the racetrack, and the last relay will decide the outcome of the meet."

We still had a chance to win! I could almost feel the silky red ribbon being clipped to my bridle.

Gwen lined me up behind the other ponies while the ring stewards set up the props. I could see that the next game was going to be a flag race. Eager for my turn to come, I couldn't help jigging in place, even though this was poor manners.

For Pony Club, for glory! as old Huw would say.

2

Flag Race

The rules were simple. In each team's lane, three empty buckets stood an equal distance apart along the meadow. At the end was a barrel with three orange flags resting on top. Our riders had to circle the barrel from a full gallop and grab the flags with one hand while guiding us with the other. On the way home, they had to drop a flag into each bucket.

Bang! went the starter's gun, and Glenn urged Eryl into a gallop. The first three legs of the race went by in a blur. I trembled with pent-up excitement, waiting for Snowdrop to cross the finish line. Finally Gwen released my reins and we were off!

The Eridge Hunt team was half a lap ahead. At the end of the meadow, Susan swept Apricot into a tight turn around the barrel and snatched up her flags. A few seconds later I reached my own barrel, circling it so tightly that my haunches brushed the rounded edge. It rocked slightly but didn't fall.

Ahead, Susan dropped her first flag into the bucket.

As we approached ours, Gwen leaned so far over my right shoulder that I felt her foot come out of the stirrup on the other side. I was afraid she would fall. But I heard the flag drop into the bucket, and she regained her balance. The Carmarthenshire team was cheering wildly, but I was sure that even a real racehorse couldn't catch up now. Eridge Hunt was just too far ahead.

Then Susan misjudged the distance and let go of her next flag a split second too late. She had to dismount and drop it into the bucket from the ground. By the time she was back on track, Apricot and I were once again running neck and neck.

The final bucket came up fast. Our riders leaned low over our shoulders. Two flags clattered neatly into the buckets.

Apricot's long legs flashed so fast they were a blur—but I think I wanted it just a little bit more. I pulled ahead by a nose and kept the lead as we swept across the finish line.

Winning that race felt sweeter than a bite of the reddest, ripest apple. The whole Pony Club surrounded us and gave three cheers.

Rowena reminded the riders that even champion ponies needed cooling out. Gwen hopped down from my back and loosened my sweaty girth. She ran up my stirrups and walked me in circles around the field, chatting with some Pony Clubbers from the other teams who were doing the same. I was thirsty, but Gwen gave me a drink only after she'd felt my chest to make sure it was cool and dry.

After the ponies were walked out, the riders polished their dusty boots with clean rags, straightened their ponies' tack, and mounted again for the awards lineup.

"Congratulations to the Carmarthenshire Pony Club, winner of today's gymkhana!" said the judge, who was the district commissioner of the Eridge Hunt club. She clipped one of the red rosettes onto my bridle. I tossed my head to make the ribbon flutter and flash in the sun.

Susan rode over and shook hands with Gwen. The girls were rivals, too, but also friends.

Apricot bobbed her head in congratulations, and I noticed how perfectly her mane was braided. Would Gwen and I ever be that polished?

Good show, said Apricot. *I hope I'll see you at the jump rally next month.*

Why wouldn't you? I asked, puzzled. Eridge Hunt never seemed to miss an event.

Haven't you heard? said Apricot. *There's probably going to be a war. It seems that the lead stallion of the British humans—the prime minister, they call him—is challenging some other herd called the Germans that has gotten out of control.*

Apricot always seemed to know things the other ponies didn't, because she was stabled with valuable fox hunters who traveled all over Europe. If she said the humans were going to fight, they probably were.

I had never seen such a thing before. I couldn't imagine it.

The ride home took several hours. The trailer was meant for six full-sized horses, but it could fit nine ponies in a pinch. Arian had to be loaded last so that if he kicked, he would hit the padded wall of the trailer and not one of us.

When we reached Carmarthenshire, Rowena dropped off Luc and Arian at their fine country house. Then she unloaded Nan and Arthur at their stone cottage and stone-walled field, Catrin and Seren at their farm, and the Kiffin ponies at their run-down stable yard near town. Finally we drove up into the hills, to the farmhouse where Gwen lived with her parents.

I was glad to be led into my cozy stall, bedded with sweet-smelling straw. It had a plaque on the door that said CADWGAN PASG LILI. That's my registered name. It means "Easter Lily," for I was born on Easter morning. My dam is Cadwgan Lady Lilian, and my sire is Cadwgan Starfire.

I was foaled on the Cadwgan Estate in Pembrokeshire, in a grand stable where my hooves echoed on the flagstones. Dozens of mares and foals roamed the acres of pasture, along with several breeding stallions. The grandchildren of the Earl of Cadwgan hitched their favorite ponies to a tiny dogcart and drove around, often nearly running over an unwary gardener or guest.

Every summer I was taken to the Royal Welsh Show. As a weanling, I won first place in a class of fifteen fillies. My dam thought I stood out because I was a strawberry roan. My legs and head were chestnut, except for my socks and blaze, but the reddish-brown hairs on my body were mixed with white ones. From a distance, I looked almost pink. My dam always said it's the prettiest color a Welsh pony can be. Although my half sister Water Lily once told me my dam had said the same of *her*, and she was dapple-gray.

One spring, a vet from Carmarthenshire came to give the ponies their yearly shots, after our usual vet broke his leg being kicked by a cow. Of course, a Welsh pony would never kick a vet, no matter how many nasty injections he gave her. She might nip just a little, but never kick.

Welsh ponies also don't brag, but the truth is, there were many fine ponies on the Cadwgan estate that Doc Lloyd could have bought for his daughter, Gwen. But he picked me.

In the beginning, I was sad to leave my home. That year would have been my first as a broodmare. But after I met Gwen, I didn't feel as sorry about not having colts or fillies of my own. Human children are really quite charming. At times I think they're even cleverer than pony foals, as hard as that is to believe.

Gwen was eight years old then. She had two dark brown braids down her back, and she was always losing her hair ribbons. She'd learned to ride on her father's gray cob, Merlin, but that didn't compare with having a pony of her own.

"Is she really mine? Can I canter her?" she asked right away when she saw me.

Soon Gwen was not only cantering but galloping me across the countryside. When she discovered that I was a good jumper, the stone walls, streams, and hedges that divided the hills and valleys were no barrier anymore. At times

we tried to jump obstacles beyond our skill, and
Gwen led me home with her jodhpurs covered in
grass stains.

She always gave me plenty of carrots and pats,
but there were times when she rushed my grooming to get into the saddle more quickly. Sometimes she forgot to wipe down my bit, so it crusted
over with green film.

Doc Lloyd noticed that Gwen's attention to chores didn't match her zeal for riding, and he signed her up for Pony Club. With Rowena in charge, not a single muddy fetlock or slimy snaffle went unnoticed. Now, after two years of lessons, Gwen took perfect care of me. When Rowena did stable inspections, she rarely found fault with my stall, my paddock, or my tack. There was always plenty to correct in the other children's stables, especially the Kiffins'.

Gwen turned on the radio while she curried me and fed me my supper of crushed oats with a handful of alfalfa pellets. Bing Crosby songs were my favorite, and Gwen sometimes paused to dance with the broom when her favorite Billie Holiday tunes came on.

The stall across from mine was empty, so Gwen's father must have taken Merlin on a call. The family had a car, but Doc Lloyd often went on horseback if it wasn't an emergency.

"I'd take a Welsh cob over an English automobile any day," he often said.

The radio wasn't as entertaining as usual this evening. A man was speaking on and on in a voice that sounded as dull as the drone of a distant tractor. I heard the words *Prime Minister Neville Chamberlain* and *declaration of war* several times. Just as Apricot had warned.

While Gwen listened, her currying got slower and slower until it stopped. In fact, she was so distracted that she forgot to give me the apple she had promised. Nor did she hang my red rosette on the door of my stall.

Country Practice

Gwen had school the next day, and she was too busy with chores and homework to ride. I missed summer vacation, when Gwen and Rhiannon spent most of the day riding cross-country together, with rallies every weekend.

On Saturdays, Gwen normally rode the two

miles along the road to Rowena's farm for our usual lesson. But when the weekend came, she spent the day in the backyard with her parents instead.

First, they dug a big hole in the lawn. They put rippled sheets of metal into the pit, and one on top for a roof. All together, they formed a kind of box. The family shoveled the dirt back on top, so that only a small doorway peeked out of the ground. They called this thing an "Anderson shelter."

They look like rabbits digging a warren to escape a hard winter, said Merlin as we hung our heads over the paddock gate to watch.

But it's September, I pointed out. *And they already have a house.*

That evening, a wailing sound filled the air. Although the noise was coming from far away, it was very loud. Merlin and I began to trot in nervous circles around our paddock, until Doc Lloyd caught us and shut us into our stalls. I had hay and water, but I didn't touch either. What was going on?

Then, through the window, I saw something that frightened me more than anything I had ever seen.

Three strange creatures came out of Gwen's house. From the neck down, they looked like Gwen, Doc Lloyd, and Gwen's mother, Elin. But they had big black heads with long snouts and bulging, reflective eyes, like giant flies.

The thing that looked like Gwen carried the

family's corgi, Trystan, in its arms. The creatures went into the Anderson shelter and shut the door.

I stood in the corner of my stall and trembled. The wailing went on. Finally, near dusk, it stopped. The door to the shelter opened.

Out of it came Doc Lloyd, and Gwen, and her mother. They looked just as they usually did, and they carried the heads of the giant blackflies in their hands!

Gwen and her father came into the stable to check on us. "I hate gas masks," Gwen said to her father, setting the thing down on a straw bale. "They make the air taste like rubber."

Gwen entered my stall and gave me a reassuring pat. There was a strange smell on her hands, like burning tires. Even so, I couldn't help calming down now that she was here.

"Trystan can come into the shelter with us, but Lily and Merlin can't," said Gwen. "What will we do if there's a real air raid instead of a drill? Are there gas masks for ponies?"

"No, Gwen," said Doc Lloyd. "All we will be able to do then is pray."

Gwen's mother hung dark curtains in all the windows of their house, and the windows of my stable were covered as well. Gwen went to school as usual, but there were no more Pony Club meetings. Instead, she started going out with her father on vet calls.

Doc Lloyd often sang while we rode. He was in the town choir, and his rich baritone voice lightened my step.

"Someday I'll be a vet, too," Gwen told her

father as we wended our way through the hills above the town nestled in the valley below.

"Country practice is a tough life, *annwyl*," said Doc Lloyd.

"Yes," said Gwen. "But I'm tough, too."

Our first call was to the Jones dairy farm. The milk cart was just leaving when we arrived. Gwen hopped down from my back and opened the heavy four-bar gate, waving to the milkman as he passed.

The inside of the dairy barn didn't look like any I had seen before. There was gleaming metal everywhere. The cows stood in narrow stalls with milk flowing through clear tubes attached to their udders.

"We put in the automatic milking system over the summer," said Mr. Jones. "With the Milk

Board's new minimum price per gallon, it's nearly paid for itself already."

He led the way down the aisle to a sturdy-looking Welsh Black heifer.

"She's been fussy at milking time," the farmer explained as Doc Lloyd bent down to examine the cow's udder.

"Looks like mastitis," said Doc Lloyd. Without being told, Gwen looked through her father's veterinary kit and found some ointment and anti-biotic tablets.

"There's been a lot of sore udders since we started machine-milking," said Mr. Jones. He took the medicine from Gwen. "But if those extra gallons make the difference between folks having enough to eat or going hungry during the war, I guess that's just the price of progress."

Our second call took us to the edge of town. I was surprised to find a pony in the small garden patch, standing between some bean plants and a line of laundry left out to dry. His coat was yellowed with age, like old newspaper, and he coughed painfully with every breath.

The pony's owner, a man with a fringe of gray hair, was coughing, too. "I had eight pit ponies in the forty years I worked for the mines," he said, "and I reckon old Badger was the best of them." He rested a gnarled hand on the pony's back.

Doc Lloyd treated Badger with an injection. His owner, whose name was Peter Morgan, invited Doc and Gwen inside for a cup of tea.

Merlin and I stayed outside in the garden with Badger, of course. After a few minutes, he

began to breathe more easily, and he told us about his life in the colliery works.

I was four years old when I went into the mines, he said. *I was blindfolded and lifted into the air with a crane, then lowered down the mine-shaft elevator. The stables were deep under the earth, far from the sun. Each pony had a pit boy who looked after us. It was hard work, pulling the heavy carts filled with coal.*

In some tunnels, the ceiling was so low that it scraped the fur off our backs, Badger went on. *Once, I felt a trembling deep in the earth, and I refused to go farther. But Peter didn't know. He kept cracking his whip. Then there was a great crash, and the roof of the tunnel not ten paces ahead collapsed in a shower of dirt and rocks. Peter always listened to me after that.*

The night before a show, Gwen would lock me into my stall after I had my bath. It always made me restless. I couldn't imagine being shut away from the outdoors for my whole life.

Every year, all the pit ponies got a week's vacation aboveground, said Badger. *But to tell you the truth, the sun always hurt my eyes. I lived most of my life underground. I suppose I'll always think of it as home.*

Badger was coughing only a little now, and he said the pain was less. Before we left, Doc Lloyd showed Peter how to apply a poultice to Badger's chest. He said the pony's lungs would never fully heal, but he could be made more comfortable.

"That's the important thing," said Peter. "All the pit ponies are supposed to get a proper retirement by the mining company. The truth is, many end up in the slaughterhouse after a life of service. But Badger will always have a share of my pension here."

For as long as I could remember, I had felt that life was a bit unfair because I was an "easy keeper" and was given less feed than Merlin, who got a half cup of cracked corn in addition to his oats and pellets.

But Badger's story made me realize I was a lucky pony indeed. After hearing it, I never again rattled on my empty tub when I had finished my supper and Merlin was still eating.

Night Call

Winter came, and a blanket of snow covered my paddock. I spent most of the time in my stall, with the straw piled thick and shored up against the wooden walls to help keep in the heat. Tucked into my favorite plaid stable blanket on the coldest nights, I felt as snug as a bear in hibernation.

In December, Gwen and I rode down the sparkling frosty road to Rowena's farm for a Christmas party. The children decided that I was the most sensible of all the ponies, so I was chosen to be hitched up to the old sleigh they found in Rowena's barn. Being driven wasn't so different from being ridden, and I soon adjusted to the slower, heavier signals from the driving reins. A few times the snowdrifts gave way into an unexpected ditch, and the Pony Clubbers had to dig me out.

Gwen and Rhiannon always exchanged Christmas presents. This year Gwen's gift to Rhiannon was a jingle-bell charm for Cadfael's bridle. Rhiannon gave Gwen a pair of mittens she had knitted herself. She wasn't much better at knitting than she was at braiding. Still, Gwen put the gloves on right away and hardly took them off all winter.

By February, the snow had melted into a thick, sticky mud that sucked the iron shoes right off my hooves. Late one night, I was awakened by the screech of the barn door sliding open. The beam of a flashlight shone into the stable. Doc Lloyd came in, dressed in his heavy mackintosh coat and carrying his veterinary kit.

He set his flashlight down on the ledge of Merlin's stall door. My stablemate's eyes glinted strangely in the bright beam while Doc Lloyd tacked him up.

"Dad?" called a voice from the barn doorway. "I saw a light in the yard. Is something wrong with the horses?"

"No, *annwyl*," Doc Lloyd said to Gwen. "I've

been called to a lambing at Owen Llewellyn's. The car's out of petrol, so I'll have to ride over."

"Can I come with you?" asked Gwen. And then, before her father could answer, "Please? I haven't got school tomorrow."

"Very well," Doc Lloyd agreed. "But let's hope we can sneak back in later without your mum waking up. She'd tan my hide if she knew I let you go out in this weather."

Gwen took off her mittens long enough to warm the icy metal of my bit with her hands. When she led me out of the stable, I was surprised by how *dark* everything looked. Not a single lamp was lit in the valley, and the streetlights had been put out.

When we got to the Llewellyn farm, Gwen and Doc Lloyd dismounted and led us into the barn. Inside, the air was steamy and warm from the heat of the animals. Each low wooden pen held half a dozen Llanwenog sheep. They had fluffy white bodies and delicate black legs and heads. It was still so early in the season that only a few had lambs at their sides.

Owen Llewellyn was waiting in one of the pens, along with a very round ewe who was lying on her side and clearly straining.

"I see you're traveling in style tonight," said Owen. He smiled at Gwen despite the lines of worry on his brow. "You know, that's one of the prettiest ponies I ever did see. Just the color of the rose quartz we mined from the quarry in Glamorgan when I was a lad."

"Thank you, Mr. Llewellyn." Gwen tethered Merlin and me to brass rings on the wall while her father hurried over to look at the ewe.

Owen's big black hunter, Bron, was stabled across the aisle in a box stall with higher and sturdier walls than the sheep pens. He whinnied to us in greeting.

It's nice to have company, he said. *With hunting season over, I hardly ever see other horses, and sheep*

are such dull conversation. Of course, now there's Bridget, but she's not much better.

Who's Bridget? I asked.

A girl from London, around your rider's age, said Bron. They've been sending children here to the countryside to escape the war. Meredith and Owen haven't got any of their own, so they offered to take

one in. Too bad they picked a rotten cabbage, so to speak.

I wanted to know more, but the poor ewe's bleating was drowning out our conversation. Doc Lloyd had lathered his arms with soap and water and was feeling carefully inside the ewe to figure out why she couldn't pass her lambs.

"Twins for sure," he said, beads of sweat breaking out on his brow despite the chilly air. "Wait, there's too many hooves—it's triplets!"

Owen didn't look happy at this news.

"I'm afraid they're packed in too tightly for me to untangle all those legs," said Doc Lloyd. "They'll have to be delivered by Cesarean, but I haven't got my instruments. I'll need to ride back for them."

The lines on Owen's forehead deepened. "Do

you think they'll make it till then? The birthing sac broke over an hour ago. They're probably just about suffocating."

The poor ewe wasn't even trying to push out the lambs anymore. Her eyes were glazed, and she panted with each breath.

"Yes, they need to get out into the fresh air," Doc Lloyd agreed. "Twins I can usually straighten out, but triplets . . ." He shook his head. "There's just no other way. Unless . . ."

"Unless someone with smaller hands were to try?" asked Gwen from the corner where she'd been watching.

Doc Lloyd and Owen turned to her in surprise.

"I can do it, Dad!" said Gwen. "I've watched you deliver lambs before."

Owen looked doubtful. "I think we'd best

hurry and get on with the Cesarean," he said. "If we're going to save any of them, there's no time to waste."

"How were the lambs laid out?" Gwen asked her father in a matter-of-fact voice. "Is the one closest to the birth canal in the breech position? Because if we can turn that one around, untangling the other two will be much easier."

"Yes, the first one is breech," said Doc Lloyd, looking thoughtful. "And I think you're right. It's the first lamb that's blocking the other two."

"You really think the lass can sort them out?" asked Owen. He still sounded uncertain, but there was a gleam of hope in his eyes.

"It's worth a try, Owen. And as you said, there's no time to waste."

"All right, Gwen, go ahead," said Owen.

Gwen soaped her arms like her father had done. She was still wearing her striped pajamas beneath her jacket.

"It's like a jigsaw puzzle," she said, feeling the position of the lambs. "The first one's foreleg is hooked right around the neck of the second."

Merlin and I were so busy watching the lambing that we hardly noticed a scuffling from the rafters above. Then, without warning, something landed on my back!

Tiny needles stabbed the roundest part of my hindquarters. I squealed and bucked instinctively. Something small and fuzzy landed in the straw near my hooves.

Gwen looked at me, concerned, but she couldn't leave the ewe. Owen hurried over to calm me instead.

"Danged kittens!" he said, scooping a tiny tabby out of the straw. I sniffed it curiously, no longer afraid. The kitten mewled as my breath whooshed over its dandelion-soft fur.

Just then Gwen let out a cry of triumph. She sat back on her heels, and soon a dark, wet lamb had slid out into the straw. Owen put the kitten aside and dragged the frail-looking lamb toward its mother's head so she could lick it with her rough tongue.

Gwen didn't even need to help the ewe with the other lambs. Within minutes, they had both entered the world. But one of them didn't stir, and its eyes were closed.

"Oh, it's not breathing!" said Gwen.

She took a handful of straw and rubbed the lamb all over. For a minute, nothing happened.

Then I saw the lamb's nostrils twitch. Its ribs moved faintly up and down. Then its eyes opened. Within minutes, the third lamb was struggling to its feet.

Doc Lloyd and Gwen stayed until the ewe had risen, too, and the triplets were nursing in turn.

Owen shook Gwen's hand. "It would have been a big loss to me if those lambs or their mother had died," he said. "It's a lucky thing the vet had his assistant along tonight."

On the windswept ride home, Doc Lloyd sang a folk song, "Dacw 'Nghariad." I could tell it was in Welsh, for the sound of the two languages was quite different.

Gwen didn't join in as she often did. Her teeth were chattering, and she shivered in the saddle.

"We can't even have hot chocolate when we get home," she complained. "They were out of it at the store. I hope we win the war soon—then there'll be plenty of chocolate in the shops, and petrol for the car."

"We are lucky if the lack of chocolate and petrol is the worst of our problems," Doc Lloyd replied.

"If the Germans win the war, will you still be a vet?" asked Gwen in a small voice. "Will there still be a Pony Club?"

"No, *annwyl*, I don't imagine so. But I believe we will win, because we've got right on our side."

By the time we got home, the sky had brightened into morning. Shoots of tender grass had pushed through the mud in the corner of my paddock, and a rosy-throated bluebird chirped in the branches of the crab apple tree.

Despite the chill that lingered in the air, it was beginning to feel like spring.

Bridget the Brat

Pony Club did start up again in March, even though the war went on. But a few things had changed.

"There will be no rallies with other districts," said Rowena. "It's too dangerous to travel with the ponies, and a waste of fuel. However, that means we can devote all the more time to studying our Pony Club manuals and learning good stable management and equitation."

None of the children looked very excited at this news.

"I heard that soap might be rationed soon," said Rhiannon, sounding hopeful. "If it is, do we still have to clean our saddles and bridles after every lesson?"

"In the event that our nation faces a saddle soap shortage, we will rely on a damp cloth and elbow grease to condition our tack," said Rowena, and Rhiannon sighed.

The biggest change to the Pony Club was its membership. Sixteen-year-old Catrin had gone to Cardiff to work in an airplane-parts factory, leaving Seren behind on her parents' farm.

A new rider had taken her place. Bridget's hair was the color of oat straw, and her eyes were as cool and gray as a winter sky. She spoke differently than the other children did, although they seemed to understand each other.

She was riding Bron, who looked even taller than I remembered. He must have stood seventeen hands, and the smaller ponies could nearly

have trotted under his belly. Bridget looked like a child's doll on his back. She wore scuffed boots that I recognized from Rowena's spare bin, and a saggy pair of jodhpurs.

Before the lesson started, Rowena asked Bridget to tell the rest of the Pony Club about herself.

"Back home, in London, my family lives in a

three-story brick town house with four servants," said Bridget. A few eyebrows began to rise.

"My father is a famous surgeon, and he lets me rent horses to hack on the commons whenever I want," she continued. "Sometimes I get invited to ride with the children of counts and duchesses. My favorite horse is a purebred Arabian mare named Fancy, and I have a special outfit just for riding: a hunter-green jacket with a pair of chocolate-brown field boots and kid leather gloves. I had to leave on the train in such a hurry that I couldn't pack my clothes, so for now I have to wear these old hand-me-downs."

By the end of this speech, the other riders were staring at Bridget as if she were a two-headed calf.

"Of course, I don't expect I'll be here long," Bridget went on, wrinkling her nose as she looked at the muddy paddocks and shaggy ponies. "England will surely win the war soon, and I can go home."

"Not soon enough," Rhiannon whispered to Gwen.

"It's not *England* fighting the war—it's *Britain*," Luc called out. "Welsh folk are part of it, too."

"Yes, but the Nazis don't care about boring old Wales," said Bridget with a sniff. "That's why they're sending children from London here, because it's not important enough to bomb."

"All right, that's enough!" said Rowena, tapping her riding crop against her boot. "Everyone, pick up a rising trot . . . and check your diagonal!"

When Gwen was on the proper diagonal, she rose slightly out of the saddle as my outside leg was striking forward, and sat down when it moved back. I could always tell when Gwen was on the right diagonal, but she often seemed to have trouble.

Now I felt her weight shift forward as she glanced at my shoulder to check. It was wrong, so she sat for two beats to switch.

"Try not to look down, Gwen," Rowena corrected. "You should be able to *feel* if you're on the right diagonal."

Gwen brought me back to a walk, then picked up the trot and tried again. This time she got it right without looking down.

Across the ring, Bridget was having trouble with Bron. He was trotting too fast and leaning heavily on the reins. Bridget's pale cheeks were flushed, and her arms looked like lead weights attached to Bron's reins as he pulled.

Rowena called for the riders to drop their stirrups. Bron leaped forward when he felt the empty irons banging against his sides, and nearly crashed into Rhiannon and Cadfael.

Instead of apologizing, Bridget shrieked, "Get that fat pony out of my way!"

When Bridget got mad, her face turned red and scrunched up. I thought she looked exactly like a dried apple that had been left sitting in the bin too long.

Rhiannon's mouth dropped open, but nothing came out. It didn't matter, because Bridget went on. "It's too bad that half your club rides such ragamuffin ponies," she said loudly. Her gaze lingered on each of the Kiffin mounts. "I guess you don't win much at shows unless the other teams' ponies are even worse."

"That's not true!" cried Rhiannon. "We took first prize at the last meet. Anyway, I'll bet your precious Fancy's nothing special, or she wouldn't be rented out for rides in the park. In fact, I bet you're making it all up. Maybe there is no Fancy, and your father isn't even a surgeon. I bet he's . . . a lorry driver, or he has no job at all and is on the dole!"

By now everyone had forgotten about the lesson. The riders let their reins grow slack as we ponies milled aimlessly around the arena. Then Rowena came to her senses.

"I thought I told everyone to drop their stirrups and trot!" Her voice boomed louder than a show announcer's megaphone.

All the riders obeyed at once, even Bridget.

As the lesson continued, I noticed that most of the time Bridget sat very nicely on Bron. Her hands were low and steady, heels pressed down, shoulders straight. But when the hunter's sweeping strides got too fast, she began to tilt forward and clutch the reins, spooking him.

Rowena made the class walk and trot for nearly the whole lesson. We cantered one at a time, with the rest of the group halted in the center of the ring.

We often jumped for the second half of class. But today, instead of setting up fences, Rowena laid out a grid of wooden poles on the ground. Trotting over ground poles was a good way to practice lengthening and shortening stride, as Rowena adjusted the distance between them. But it wasn't as exciting as jumping.

After the lesson, Owen Llewellyn was waiting in Rowena's driveway. He greeted Bridget cheerfully and helped her load Bron into his stock trailer.

"I guess the princess is too good to ride home like the rest of us," muttered Rhiannon. It was true that the Llewellyns' farm was less than two miles away—closer than either Rhiannon's home or Gwen's.

Gwen always rode with the Kiffins up to the place where the road split. A few cars passed, but we were used to them. They didn't spook us unless they went by too fast or honked their horns.

"Can you believe how awful she is?" Rhiannon said while her brothers and sisters rode ahead. "I bet her parents are grateful to the Germans for giving them an excuse to send her away!"

"Well, she shouldn't have said that about Cadfael and the other ponies," Gwen said slowly. "But if we had to leave our homes and live with a family we'd never met, I don't think we'd be very friendly, either."

"Or maybe Bridget's just a brat no matter where she is!" said Rhiannon, and gave Cadfael a kick so that he trotted to catch up with the other ponies.

When we reached Gwen's house, her mother was digging in the garden—or what remained of it. She had replaced her beloved rosebushes with rows of cabbage and potatoes.

Trystan, who was gnawing on a pig's ear treat nearby, leaped up and capered in greeting. His stump of a tail wagged furiously. His fur was coppery orange, with a handsome white ruff around his neck. And his ears seemed twice as big as they needed to be, atop his fox-like face.

Of course, Trystan would have said they were exactly the right size, since he was always first to hear an approaching visitor or the sound of Doc Lloyd's car door opening. Now I played his favorite game with him, flattening my ears in mock fierceness and lunging forward so that he ran away, barking—only to come racing back a moment later so I could do it again.

"How was your lesson?" Elin asked her daughter, standing up and brushing the dirt from her overalls. She had shiny dark hair like Gwen's, although hers was bobbed short and waved.

"Pony Club doesn't seem as fun this year, somehow," said Gwen with a little sigh. Then her face brightened, and she patted me. "But Lily was wonderful, as usual. And I'm getting better at telling my diagonal."

A growling noise came from above. It was one of the strange birdlike things with frozen wings that often passed overhead now. Both Gwen and her mother looked anxiously up at the sky. I'd noticed people doing that often lately, as if they were expecting something worse than rain or hail to fall.

Riding Lessons

"Nan, try to keep your hands steady. Glenn and Megan, heels down. Rhiannon, stop talking to Cadfael. He speaks pony, not English. Use your legs and seat!"

This week the class was working on balance at the trot. Our riders posted for three strides and sat for three. Then they rose into two-point position for three strides, as if they were approaching a fence. Rowena's choice of schooling activities was a wise one. The steady rhythm kept the more skittish horses like Bron quiet, and the riders too focused to gossip or argue.

After the class had been working for half an hour or so, Rowena called for everyone to stop. "We don't want the ponies to get sour from too much repetition," she said. "Shall we play a game for the rest of the lesson?"

"Egg and spoon!" said Dylan.

I hoped not. Nine riders balancing raw eggs on spoons was a messy game, and I didn't like the feel of the shells crunching under my hooves.

"No, eggs are rationed now. We can't waste them," said Glenn.

"Musical chairs?" suggested Megan. But the chairs would have to be brought outside from Rowena's house, which would take too long.

"Let's play puissance!" said Luc, and there were cries of agreement.

"What's that?" asked Bridget.

"It's a competition to see who can jump the highest," said Nan. "It's great fun!"

Rowena suggested that Bridget could just watch if she wanted, but Bridget insisted that she'd jumped before, on Fancy. And maybe she had. She'd surprised everyone by showing up to the lesson dressed in the very clothes she had bragged about. Her parents had sent them on an express train from London, along with some fancy marzipan candies that she'd shared with the class.

Everyone seemed to have an improved opinion of her since then—except Rhiannon, who hadn't taken a candy.

Rowena set up a small vertical jump in the center of the arena, then dragged over a second pole and laid it at the base.

"What's that for?" asked Dylan.

"Because you always use a ground pole," said Nan.

"But why?" asked Dylan. Nan thought for a moment, then shrugged.

"Ponies' eyesight is different from ours," said Gwen, who read her father's textbooks and knew things the other children didn't. "They haven't got very good depth perception, so a ground pole helps them judge the height of the fence."

"Correct," said Rowena, looking pleased. "Now, who shall go first?"

The riders decided to go in order of age, youngest to oldest. Dylan didn't jump yet, so Nan went first. Arthur managed to heave himself over the rail, though he looked quite spent afterward, and no one else had any trouble, either. Bron looked almost sleepy as he cantered over the low fence.

I thought it was too bad that Catrin Pritchard had left the club with Seren. He was an excellent jumper. In fact, Doc Lloyd had been called to see him last week after he'd jumped out of his paddock and into some barbed wire—luckily, he hadn't been hurt badly.

Rowena raised the jump for the next round. Arthur couldn't summon the energy to clear the higher bar and knocked it down. Taffy spooked at a butterfly and bolted sideways around the wooden standards. She was out, too.

Gwen rose slightly in her stirrups as we approached the fence. At the last moment, she released the reins and rested her hands lightly on the crest of my neck. I arched my neck and back in the air and landed smoothly on the other side. The other riders murmured with approval,

and I knew we looked just like the pictures of *correct jumping form* on the poster that hung outside Rowena's tack room door.

In the next round, Megan asked Snowdrop to take off from too long a distance and had a fault. In the round after that, Arian was wearing his grumpy face because Taffy had been standing too near him, and he rapped the pole and brought it down.

Bron still hardly seemed to be jumping so much as stepping over the fence. It didn't seem fair, since his legs were so much longer than the other ponies'. Still, I had no trouble clearing the bar when my next turn came.

Cadfael was a strong jumper for such a little pony, but he was in a devilish mood. He cantered as prettily as a rocking horse up to the fence.

Then his little ears began to twitch. He tucked his hindquarters and slammed to a halt so fast that his nose bumped into the painted rail. Rhiannon went sailing over alone. Everyone winced when she hit the ground with a *thump* on the other side.

She sat up right away, looking annoyed. Rowena hurried over and made Rhiannon count her fingers and say the alphabet backward to make sure she didn't have a concussion. Meanwhile, Winnifred and Glenn headed off Cadfael as he tried to dart out the arena gate.

Oh, Caddy, one of these days Rhiannon's going to have enough of your antics and send you to the knacker, Eryl warned him.

The knacker went around to all the farms with his truck and took away old and lame animals for dog meat. I had never heard of a pony sent to the knacker for being bad. But Eryl swore it could happen and that Cadfael's turn would soon come.

Rhiannon wasn't hurt, so she got back on and made Cadfael jump the fence properly. She didn't seem upset by the fall. I think she secretly enjoyed having the naughtiest pony.

They were eliminated, of course, so now it was just Eryl, Bron, and me. Eryl was tall and graceful, but her shin splints made her weak in the leg. She knocked down the pole in the next round.

Now the fence was over a meter high, and Bron seemed to have decided that it qualified as a real jump. His strides grew faster and faster, swallowing up the ground. He jumped higher than he needed to and kicked up his heels when he landed.

"Get his head up!" called Rowena, for a horse could buck only with his head down between his knees. Bridget managed to get Bron back under control, but she looked pale and shaken.

Rowena raised the fence. It was now higher than anything I had jumped before.

This time I had trouble seeing the spot where I should take off. Three strides would bring me too close to the fence, but two—no, that was impossibly far. I couldn't make it!

I hesitated, chipped in a third stride, and didn't have enough power to clear the fence. My front legs smacked into the pole and brought it crashing down.

Gwen patted me anyway and told me I had done well. I was still disappointed, and my cannon bones smarted from hitting the rail.

"If Bridget goes clear this round, she wins!" cried Nan from the sidelines, where everyone who had been eliminated was watching.

Bron was getting quite "hot," bouncing into little rears on his hind legs and tossing his head. This only made Bridget choke up on the reins even more. Frustrated, Bron grabbed the bit in his teeth and bolted toward the jump.

He took off in a massive leap. Bridget clung to his neck like a burr stuck in his mane. When they landed, Bridget was jolted out of the saddle and landed in a heap on the ground.

Bron halted right away and lowered his head, looking ashamed. I knew he hadn't thrown her on purpose. He had only been overexcited.

Bridget sprang to her feet. She looked down at her fancy clothes, now dirty and torn. Before anyone could do anything to help her, she grabbed Bron's trailing reins and smacked him with her riding crop, hard.

"Stupid horse, you've ruined everything!" She smacked him again.

Bron cowered back on his haunches, his eyes wide with fright. Bridget threw the reins on the ground and stormed out of the arena, around the corner of the big red barn, and out of sight.

The Pony Club was speechless. Even Rowena looked stunned.

Then she went over to Bron, gathered his reins, and spoke to him in a reassuring voice. His worried look faded quickly. He had always been treated well, and he'd been more surprised than hurt by Bridget's blows.

"Riders, please walk out your horses for fifteen

minutes, then return to the stable," said Rowena. She loosened Bron's girth, ran up his stirrups, and led him out of the ring in the direction Bridget had gone.

I bet she won't be allowed in Pony Club anymore, said Cadfael as Rhiannon crossed the ring so that she and Gwen could walk side by side. *Rowena hates when anyone loses their temper with a horse.*

I thought this was a lucky thing for Cadfael, who often acted much naughtier than Bron had. But indeed, both horse and rider were gone by the time the rest of the class entered the stable yard. Rowena's matched pair of Shires, Lady and Pip, trotted across their pasture to greet us. They hung their massive heads over the fence to have their foreheads scratched.

When Nan timidly asked whether Bridget

would be coming back, Rowena only set her lips in a thin line and said, "That remains to be seen."

The day was far from over for the rest of the Pony Clubbers. Our riders tethered us to the paddock fence with safety-release knots that could be pulled loose quickly if we started to panic. Except clever Cadfael had figured out how to free himself by grabbing the end of the lead with his teeth, so Rhiannon had to keep a close eye on him.

After they untacked us, the children divided a bale of hay into flakes. They scattered the piles far enough apart that the greedier ponies—I would never behave so rudely, of course—didn't chase the others away and hoard it all.

While we ponies ate our lunch, the Pony Clubbers cleaned their tack. They removed the stirrup leathers from their saddles, took apart their bridles, and rubbed the leather with a damp sponge dipped in saddle soap. Slowly, the dust and sweat were polished away. Then the children laid the pieces on clean feed sacks to dry and took a break for their own tea.

"Not a dried-egg sandwich again," complained Rhiannon, peering into her paper bag with dismay.

Gwen looked guiltily down at her own sandwich, which was full of crispy bacon, tomato, and slices of cheese. Since so many farmers were grateful to Doc Lloyd for saving their animals, the family never lacked the fresh eggs and meat that had grown scarce since the war.

Gwen also had a piece of apple cake. She often gave me half of her dessert, but today she shared with Rhiannon instead.

After lunch, the riders put their clean tack

back together. Dylan and Nan kept buckling the wrong pieces until Gwen helped them. She taught the younger children a song she had made up to remember which pieces attached to which.

"I forgot how nice and peaceful Pony Club is without Bridget," said Rhiannon while the riders got ready to go home. "I hope she's gone for good."

"I guess so," said Gwen reluctantly. "It was wrong of her to hit Bron like that. But maybe if she had a second chance . . ."

"You always see the best in everything, don't you?" said Rhiannon, giving Gwen a look that was half friendly, half annoyed.

Bridget did return to Pony Club the next week, and Rowena made it clear that nobody was to speak of the last lesson.

"I think we can all remember mistakes we've made," she said sternly. Nine riders flushed, recalling times they had yanked on their pony's reins in frustration or forgotten to latch a gate. I wondered if Gwen was thinking of the day she'd been in such a hurry to ride that she skipped picking out my hooves, and I'd gotten a stone bruise.

"That's why we take riding lessons," said Rowena. "To learn."

Bron didn't seem to hold a grudge against Bridget, but the Pony Club riders weren't so forgiving. As the weeks passed, I often heard the children mocking her in an exaggerated English accent. Sometimes they switched to speaking Welsh when she came near. Gwen never made fun of Bridget, but Rhiannon sulked whenever Gwen tried to talk to her, so she rarely did.

Bridget mostly kept to herself and focused on her riding. Bron still rushed over fences, but his flat work was much better already. Bridget got him to arch his neck and go "on the bit" in a way that Rowena said the rest of the class should strive for. Rowena pointed out how Cadfael, in particular, went around with his back hollow and his nose sticking up in the air. Although this comparison might have been helpful for the children's equitation, it only caused Rhiannon to like Bridget even less.

But Rowena soon made an announcement that left everyone too excited to bicker. In spite of the war, the Carmarthenshire Pony Club was going to host a horse show!

It would be held at Rowena's farm, and the Eridge Hunt and South Notts riders were invited.

The entry fees, along with profits from a bake sale and a raffle, would benefit the Red Cross.

Best of all, there would be a Pony Jumper championship—the class Apricot had won last year. The prize was not only a rosette but a special trophy, too.

Rowena always said that Pony Club spirit was more important than ribbons and awards. Most of the time, I agreed. But all that went out of my head as soon as I heard about the show.

I wanted to win that Pony Jumper trophy more than anything in the world.

Pony Swap

The show was held on Easter Sunday. Many of the spectators arrived after church, in their best suits and flowery spring dresses. The Pony Clubbers had set up a big white tent in Rowena's field, with an elegant luncheon table loaded with sandwiches and desserts.

The other parents had pooled their butter and sugar rations so Gwen's mother could bake a giant batch of her famous Welsh cakes. Crispy outside, soft inside, and studded with juicy currants, they were my favorite treat. I hoped Gwen would remember to give me one later. It *was* my birthday, after all.

The first class on the program, Tack and Turnout, was unmounted. The weather was too cool for Gwen to give me a bath, but she had brushed me to a shine, combed my mane and tail free of tangles, and coated my hooves with clear polish. She had even borrowed her father's razor to shave my whiskers.

Still, the worn leather of my saddle and bridle didn't gleam like the beautiful reddish-mahogany tack worn by Apricot. Although Gwen's boots and Pony Club pin were perfectly polished, the sleeves of her show jacket were a bit too short this year.

Nobody was surprised when Apricot and Susan won the class. Arian and Luc took the blue ribbon for second. Luc's father was a wealthy quarry owner, so Luc always had new clothes and tack. And Luc's mother always braided Arian for him, which I felt was cheating.

The second class, Equitation, judged the rider's form. Gwen and I took second place . . . to Apricot, once again. In the third class, Pleasure—which judged the horse's way of going—Gwen and I placed first, ahead of Apricot. But it was the Pony Jumper that I really cared about winning!

I would have to wait, though, because jumping classes were always held at the end of the day.

After the Pleasure ribbons were awarded, Rowena announced a surprise class: a Pony Swap. Everyone murmured with excitement at the news. Rowena often said that a good rider could ride any horse well, but she'd never made the children trade off before.

The children drew slips of colored paper from a riding hat. The two who got the same color would swap. Gwen drew a green slip. She looked around to see who else had one. It was Bridget!

Poor Bridget and Bron hadn't won any ribbons at all. In Tack and Turnout, Bridget had forgotten to put the ends of her bridle straps in their keepers. She also hadn't braided Bron's mane, as was proper at a fancy show like this.

In Equitation, Bron had fallen back into his habit of rushing at the trot. In Pleasure, Bridget had kept him under such a tight rein that he looked like a coiled spring ready to explode. This seemed odd, because they had been going so well together in lessons. I'd even thought they might be competition for the top prizes.

Gwen said "Good luck!" to Bridget as they swapped reins, but the other girl didn't answer. Her eyes looked strange today, red and puffy, like Gwen's during ragweed season.

Bridget was a bit taller than Gwen, so she lenghthened my stirrups two holes before she mounted. She sat more forward in the saddle than Gwen, and her hands were lighter on the reins. They felt almost like cobwebs attached to my bit instead of leather.

At first it hardly seemed like I had a rider on my back at all. But soon I discovered that guidance came in the form of slight pressure from Bridget's hands and heels. I even started to enjoy her soft touch. I relaxed into an elastic trot, then a lively canter as the judge called for a change of gaits.

Bron seemed to appreciate Gwen's firmer signals. Gwen kept her balance posting to his big trot and sat his canter well. Watching them, I felt just the tiniest bit jealous, and I tried to go even more prettily for Bridget. At the end of the class, we stood in line while the runner brought in the ribbons.

I was pleased—and not entirely surprised, for I really had been lovely—when the judge called out Bridget's name for first prize.

Cadfael, who'd been unusually angelic for Susan, took second. A South Notts rider on an Eridge Hunt horse took third, and Rhiannon placed fourth with Apricot. Gwen was fifth on Bron, who'd picked up a wrong lead at the canter.

Outside the arena, Bridget slid down from my back, stroking and praising me. For a moment her face seemed light and happy, like a child's should. Then it clouded over again. She looked down at the red rosette in her hand and crushed it in her gloved fist.

"Congratulations," said Gwen, leading Bron over. "You did well on Lily."

Bridget glared at her. "Your silly pink pony is so quiet that a toddler could ride her," she snapped. "No wonder you win all the time. I guess now you can see that it's not so easy on a *real* horse." She grabbed Bron's reins from Gwen and stalked off.

"See, it's no use being nice to her," said Rhiannon, who was back on Cadfael and scolding him for behaving better for his borrowed rider than he did for her.

Gwen's face was flushed from Bridget's unkind words. "I wonder if it's true," she said, "that I only do well in shows because Lily is so gentle and well trained."

"Maybe, but *you're* the one who trained her," Rhiannon pointed out.

After the Pony Swap was a short break while fences were set up for the jumping classes. The Welsh cakes were fast disappearing from the luncheon table, and Gwen paused to stuff a few into her jacket pocket for later.

The lowest jumping class, Crossrails, had just started. Gwen led me over to the rail to cheer on Nan and Arthur. The Pony Jumper championship was next, and I felt confident. I had beaten Apricot once today, and I could beat her again.

After watching a few more rounds, Gwen brought me to the practice arena to warm up over some fences. As she was trotting me toward a low vertical, her stirrup leather broke. The iron struck my hoof with a clang and bounced away into the dirt.

Gwen fell forward onto my neck but quickly

regained her balance. Lucky thing it hadn't happened in the air over a fence—Gwen could have been badly hurt!

"Are you okay?" called Rhiannon from across the arena.

"Yes," said Gwen, hopping down and looking at the ragged ends of the worn leathers. "I should have replaced these ages ago. Everything's just so expensive now that I didn't want to ask my parents."

Gwen led me to the barn to borrow an extra pair from Rowena's spare tack trunk. As we rounded the corner, I noticed Bridget and Bron cantering alone across the back pasture, toward the Brechfa woods.

I whinnied to Bron. Gwen looked up and saw them, too. Quickly, she finished fixing her stirrup

and swung up onto my back. But she didn't turn
me toward the arena, where the fences were being
raised for the Pony Jumper championship.

She was asking me to go into the woods after
Bridget and Bron.

Maybe if I ignored her and cantered back
to the showground instead, Gwen would forget
about them and remember our class. But Gwen
gave me another squeeze with her heels, a clear

signal to follow Bron. I had never disobeyed her before. . . .

"Walk on, Lily," said Gwen as I balked and backed up a few steps.

I craned my neck toward the arena, with its beautifully painted jumps and flower boxes. I could even see the trophy sparkling on the judges'- table in the white tent, waiting to be presented to the winner. . . .

A third time, Gwen asked me to walk on. She tapped me lightly with her riding crop, something she hardly ever did. There could be no doubt what she was asking of me.

I lowered my head and began to walk toward the woods just as the show announcer said, "*Riders, gather at the arena gate. The Pony Jumper championship is about to begin!*"

An Ideal Pony

Bridget and Bron were already out of sight, but my sensitive ears had no trouble telling which way they'd gone. When the trail split, Gwen gave me my head and let me choose which path to take. Wherever the trail was clear enough, I trotted or cantered to catch up.

In a few minutes, I caught sight of Bron in a clearing ahead. His saddle was empty, and at first I thought Bridget had fallen. Then I saw her sitting on the mossy bank of a stream, with bell-shaped white lily-of-the-valley flowers blooming all around her.

Bron's reins were looped carelessly over a tree branch. Gwen dismounted at once and called out

to Bridget in a sharp tone, "That's not the right way to tie up a horse, you know!"

Bridget looked up, startled. Tears were streaming down her cheeks.

"What's the matter?" asked Gwen in a softer voice.

For a moment, Bridget didn't speak. She picked one of the lily-of-the-valley blossoms, tore

off its petals one by one, and dropped them into the swift current.

"I got a telegram this morning that my father was hurt by a German bomb," she said finally. "Somewhere in Scotland, at a naval base, where he was training other surgeons to operate on wounded soldiers."

Gwen's eyes got very wide. She tied Bron the correct way, unbuckling the reins from his bit and attaching them to his noseband instead so he wouldn't hurt his mouth if he pulled back. She did the same for me, then went over to Bridget, stepping carefully to avoid crushing any of the flowers.

"He's back in London now, but I can't go see him," said Bridget as Gwen sat beside her at the stream's edge. "Everyone is saying that the Axis armies will probably attack the city as soon as they can gather their forces."

Bridget scraped some moss off a rock with the toe of her riding boot. "In the Pony Swap class, I was having so much fun on Lily that, for a few minutes, I forgot that my dad is lying in a hospital bed, and the Germans could bomb the telegraph office where my mum works. If something happens to one of them, I might not even hear about it for days."

Now Gwen's eyes were filled with tears as well.

"What if our home is destroyed, or the park where I ride? And Fancy . . ." Bridget's voice trailed off.

"I'm sorry," Gwen said softly. "I always say that ponies fix everything, but I guess even they can't make the war end."

For a minute the girls stared silently into the water.

"I didn't want to go to the show at all this morning, but Owen and Meredith said it might be the best distraction," said Bridget. "I guess it worked for a while. . . ."

"You really were wonderful on Lily," said Gwen. "She is quiet, but only if she likes you. And she's not pink, by the way. She's a strawberry roan."

"It's a pretty color." Bridget wiped her cheek on the arm of her hunter-green jacket, which Meredith had mended after her fall. "I just wish my parents were here so they could see how much better my riding has gotten, now that I can practice every day," she said. Then she scowled. "No,

I wish this rotten war was over and I could go home!"

This time she plucked not a flower but a big penny bun mushroom from the bank and flung it into the water. The splash startled Bron, and he jumped and rolled his eyes in her direction.

"Everyone makes fun of my accent, and sheep are so stupid," she went on. "Every time I see one, I want to kick it!"

Suddenly Bridget was pouting again, looking as bratty as ever, with the same wrinkly dried-apple expression on her face.

Gwen just stared at her for a moment. Then she burst into laughter. "You s-sound as if you hate sh-sheep more than you hate the Nazis," she said, breathless with giggles.

At first Bridget pouted even harder. Then she started laughing, too. "Maybe we should drop sheep instead of bombs on the Germans."

"*Baaaa!*" said Gwen, and the girls dissolved into merriment again.

What's the matter with them? asked Bron, snorting and prancing sideways a few steps. *Were they bitten by a rabid fox?*

No, that's just the way children are sometimes, I said.

Yes, the lambs are silly, too, said Bron. *But they stop being that way when they become adult sheep. Nor is Owen Llewellyn silly when he rides me. I believe I prefer both sheep and humans when they are grown up.*

Gwen produced the folded napkin into which she'd tucked several of her mother's Welsh cakes.

"I'm starving," she said. "I haven't eaten all day. Have you?" She offered one to Bridget.

Bridget nibbled one of the cakes. "It's good," she said.

"They're Lily's favorite." Gwen looked over and noticed my nostrils wafting the air. She divided the last cake and gave half to me, half to Bron. How good it tasted!

"We should probably get back to the show," said Bridget when we'd finished our treats. She looked at Bron's high stirrup and bit her lip.

"I'll give you a leg up," offered Gwen. Bridget let Gwen boost her by the knee into Bron's saddle.

"Maybe we could do another swap for fun sometime," Gwen suggested as we walked side by side along the trail. "It's nice to try a different horse, and I'm not scared of Bron."

"I'm not scared of him, either," Bridget said quickly, patting his neck. "But I'd like to ride Lily again. She really is perfect."

She gave me an admiring glance, and I couldn't help bobbing my head with pleasure at the compliment I knew she was giving me. Of course, a Welsh pony is always modest, but there's no point in turning up your nose at a sugar lump you've earned, as my dam always said.

When we got back to the farm, the Pony Jumper class was over. Apricot had won the trophy, but somehow it didn't seem to matter as much as before.

When Rowena asked where we had been, Gwen just said that she and Bridget had taken a trail ride. Rowena accepted this with a raised eyebrow and said nothing more about it. Gwen and

Bridget stayed along with the other riders to help clean up the grounds and count the profits—more than three hundred pounds for the Red Cross.

Afterward, Gwen invited Bridget to ride home with her and the Kiffins. Rhiannon grimaced slightly, but she didn't say anything. For a few moments, there was an uncomfortable silence as the group rode together.

"Has anyone seen the latest Clark Gable film, *Gone with the Wind?*" asked Bridget. "I noticed it's playing at the cinema downtown."

Glenn rolled his eyes. "I wouldn't be caught dead watching a dumb movie like that," he said.

"I don't really like mushy romantic movies, either," said Gwen. "I like westerns!"

But Rhiannon gasped. "I love Clark Gable!" she said. "Which of his movies have you seen?"

"Only all of them!" Bridget giggled. "Even if I had to sneak into the theater."

Rhiannon looked at Bridget as if she were weighing something in her mind. "Maybe we could go see *Gone with the Wind* together," she said.

Bridget looked surprised, then a little suspicious. "Really?"

Rhiannon nodded. "None of my brothers or sisters understand the genius of Clark Gable."

"Well, all right," said Bridget, still looking startled but now pleased, too. "How about next Saturday?"

Our riders were lingering at the fork in the road when Doc Lloyd came trotting from the other direction on Merlin.

"Where are you going?" Gwen asked as he

drew near. Doc Lloyd told her that Seren had cut himself jumping out of his paddock and into the cow field next door again.

"Oh no!" said Gwen. "Why does he keep doing that?"

"I think he's lonely," replied Doc Lloyd. "With Catrin gone, nobody pays him much attention."

"Do you think Gwen and I could come with you?" asked Bridget shyly. "I've never been on a vet call before."

Doc Lloyd said he'd appreciate the company, so off we went.

And it was love at first sight. Bridget held Seren's halter while Doc Lloyd stitched up his leg. When the friendly palomino nuzzled her hand, Bridget's face broke into the biggest smile I had seen on it. "What a beautiful pony," she kept saying.

Of course, I had come to the obvious solution at once: Bridget needed a pony, and Seren a new owner. But the cleverness of a Welsh pony is a rare gift, so I tried to be patient while everyone else put the pieces together.

Gwen was the first to suggest it. "Seren really is an ideal pony for Bridget, isn't he?" she said. "Much better than Bron."

"But I couldn't ask Mr. and Mrs. Llewellyn for

my own pony," said Bridget. "I'm an unwanted guest in their home already."

"I know for a fact they don't see you that way," said Doc Lloyd. "And I think you're just what this pony needs. In fact, I'm making it my prescription. 'One little girl to apply riding and grooming daily.'"

The details were worked out easily enough. The Pritchards had no need for a pony anymore, and as Doc Lloyd had thought, Owen and Meredith were happy to buy him for Bridget. Soon enough, Seren was healed from his scrapes and settled into his new home on the Llewellyns' sheep farm.

And Bridget? Well, she looked far less like a dried apple when she smiled.

Victory!

Five more years passed, and it was hard to remember a time before the war. In some ways, not much had changed. We still had Pony Club every Saturday, unless the air raid sirens went off in town. And once or twice a year, several Pony Club chapters would get together for a games rally or a benefit show for charity.

One summer, Rowena organized a mock hunt. Rhiannon played the fox, scattering bits of confetti as "scent" for the hunt master (Gwen) and the hounds (the rest of the Pony Club) to follow.

We galloped through the fields, jumping everything in sight, until Megan spotted confetti washed up on the stream bank at the edge of the Brechfa woods. We followed that stream into the shadowy forest for more than an hour, until Bridget realized that Rhiannon had fooled us all.

The clever fox had been riding along the stream and dropping her scent into the water, where the current would carry it deeper into the woods—away from her true trail.

The hounds weren't allowed to speak during a mock hunt. Bridget could only make a yipping noise and point to the bits of confetti being swept through the water. Once Gwen figured it out, she turned the rest of the hounds right around and rode back the way we'd come.

We caught up with Rhiannon and Cadfael just as they were trotting across the field to Rowena's stable, where they would have "gone to ground" and won the game. Luckily for Cadfael, he was treated better than a real fox after we'd trapped him by the bramble patch!

Moments like this made it possible to forget our troubles for a while. But overall, life had gotten a little harder and a little leaner with each year. Hay and oats cost a lot now, since the government made farmers grow crops to feed people instead. Sadly, some owners chose to have their livestock or even family pets put to sleep rather than let them starve. Fortunately, I always had enough to eat, and so did the other Carmarthenshire ponies.

One frightening day, two officers came to town, conscripting horses for the army. They measured every horse with a stick and level, and claimed any over fifteen hands high. Merlin was just a half inch under the limit, and the officers argued about whether they should make an exception for such a sturdy-looking animal. Eventually, they left him and moved on.

But Bron was taken. Seren said they'd loaded him onto a slat-sided trailer meant for cattle, along with a dozen other horses. We later heard he was sent to a hot desert land called Palestine, where a different war was being fought.

Bridget had cried and cried over Bron, even

though she had Seren now. He had replaced Apricot as my main rival in jumping. Catrin had never really gotten the best out of the pony— perhaps she was already daydreaming about leaving for the big city. But Bridget and Seren went together like apples and oats, the perfect combination.

Of course, I rarely tasted apples now, and my portion of oats was mixed with a fair amount of chaff. In the spring and summer, Gwen rode me across the countryside to forage for rose hips, mushrooms, and wild garlic. The family even preserved the crab apples from their tree in the yard.

"Make do and mend" was a phrase I learned quickly, as it was repeated so often. It was just as well that the Pony Club didn't hold many rallies, for Gwen no longer fit into her show jacket and

jodhpurs. Now she usually rode in patched cor-
duroys and a pair of her father's old Wellington
boots.

As hard as it was to admit, Gwen's clothes
weren't the only thing she was getting too big for.
Although she was petite for fifteen, her legs hung
down to the bottom of my belly. Sadly, it's the
fate of every pony to eventually be outgrown.

Gwen was growing up in other ways, too.
Soon she would leave for a summer apprentice-
ship with a small-animal vet in Pembrokeshire.
Most practices wouldn't take a working student
so young, but Dr. Rhys had said that any daughter
of Doc Lloyd was as good as a first-year student
at the Royal Veterinary College, where Gwen
hoped to go in a few years.

Gwen explained this to me one day while she

worked at shedding out the last of my fuzzy winter coat. Then she'd laughed at herself, and I knew she was imagining Rowena saying "Speak pony, not English!" But, of course, we ponies understand more than we let on.

Even with Gwen away, I wouldn't get to spend my days lazing around and getting fat on pasture, as pleasant as that sounded. The youngest Kiffin of all, six-year-old Maisie, had started coming over after school to ride and help with the chores. She was a bright-eyed, curly-haired girl with the same wild streak as her sister Rhiannon. Gwen was teaching her to jump crossrails, and soon she would ride me in Pony Club.

This fine May afternoon, though, seemed to belong more to the past than the future. Gwen

and I were headed into town to do the family's
shopping. She had her blue ration book and her
parents' tan ones in the satchel slung across her
back.

All around us was the peaceful countryside
I knew so well, the old slate-roofed farmhouses

with victory gardens in nearly every backyard. The barns and fields were filled with horses, cattle, sheep, dogs, and cats, who'd probably all been tended by Doc Lloyd at some time in their lives.

When we reached town, Gwen tethered me in front of the grocer's shop, between the Kiffins' dented sedan and the banker's open-roofed touring car.

It seemed like Gwen was taking longer than usual with the shopping. I began to nibble on the shiny black hubcap of the banker's car to amuse myself. Then I noticed something odd.

People were drifting from shops and houses into the street, looking dazed. Gradually, their eyes met one another's and lit up, and there was much talking and embracing.

Gwen came rushing out of the store. She had

forgotten the groceries inside, but she didn't seem to notice. All around us, people were tearing down the blackout curtains and pieces of cardboard that covered the windows. Some people were even dancing in the street.

Amid this happy chaos, I gathered that a radio broadcast had announced Germany's surrender. The Allied forces had won the war!

Rhiannon's sister Winnifred came out of the cinema with her young man, Arnie, who'd escaped the draft because his arm had been crushed in a hay mower. At first they both seemed confused by the revelry. Then, when Arnie heard the news, he swept Winnifred up with his good arm and kissed her right there on the sidewalk!

Gwen giggled with delight, surely storing this juicy bit of gossip to tell Rhiannon. Since she didn't have a young man to sweep her up, she hugged me instead. Then she mounted quickly and trotted me all the way home to share the news with her family.

That night, Gwen's mother baked an apple cake in celebration, after Gwen went back to town for the forgotten groceries. And of course, Gwen made sure I got my share. It was quite tasty, even though it was made with crab apples.

A few weeks after that happy day, I stood outside sunbathing in my paddock with Merlin while Trystan enjoyed a roll in the grass nearby. Suddenly the corgi sprang to his feet and dashed to the end of the driveway, barking.

Bridget and Seren appeared on the crest of the hill. Bridget was also getting a little big for her pony, but like Gwen, she wouldn't give him up for the queen's own carriage horses.

Gwen came to the door of the surgery room at the back of the farmhouse, where she'd been helping her father. She smiled at her friend. "As soon as I've finished sterilizing these instruments, I'll come out and get Lily ready."

"For our last ride," said Bridget, looking sad.

The girls rode us through the forest to the same stream in the Brechfa woods where Gwen had comforted Bridget so many years before. Although the water was still icy, both girls took off their boots and dangled their feet in the stream.

"Did I tell you?" Bridget said to Gwen. "I'm taking Clark Gable back to London with me."

Clark Gable was the tabby kitten who'd leaped

on me from the rafters the night the triplet lambs were born. Now a plump cat, he was still in the habit of pouncing from above. For that reason, I refused to go into the barn whenever Gwen visited the Llewellyn farm.

The girls grew quiet after Bridget spoke. The lily of the valley was in bloom, and its delicate scent perfumed the air, along with the sharpness of pine needles and the earthiness of the penny bun mushrooms that still clustered at the water's edge.

A fallow deer with a dappled fawn grazed in a patch of sunlight on the far bank. Seren and I stood quietly, not even trying to graze. We were just content to be in this beautiful place.

After a time that seemed to flow by too quickly, the girls dried off their feet and got ready to go

home. Before she mounted, Gwen took something wrapped in tissue paper from her pocket and gave it to Bridget.

"This is for you, a going-away present."

Bridget unwrapped the gift. Inside was a gold pin with the image of a mounted horse and rider on a blue background, and the words *British Horse Society—Pony Club.*

"I know you didn't get one, because they stopped making them during the war," said Gwen. "But you'll still be a part of Pony Club after you go back to London, even if you don't get to ride again for a long time."

For a moment, Bridget hesitated, as if she were going to give Gwen's pin back to her. Then she closed her hand around it. "Thank you," she said softly.

"And I'll tell you what else," said Gwen, a sly smile spreading across her face.

"What?"

"I've got a couple of ration tickets for sweets that are burning a hole in my pocket. Last one to town's a rotten egg!" Gwen swung up into my saddle, and we took off cantering down the trail. Soon I heard Seren's hoofbeats behind us.

When we reached the edge of the woods, Gwen didn't steer me toward the road. Instead, she chose a shortcut that crossed half a dozen farmers' land. We had permission to ride there, but only if we left the gates exactly as they were. It would take ages to open and close them all behind us.

But we weren't going to do that. . . .

We were going up and over!

Seren caught up to us, then pulled ahead by half a length. We came closer to the big four-bar gate of the Jones farm, its shadow seeming to stretch endlessly across the ground. I had never been bold enough to jump it before—but today was the day.

Seren chipped in an extra careful stride to prepare himself, and I took off in a giant leap so that we sailed over the fence together. I felt like Pegasus, flying and free.

Maybe Rowena would have pointed out that Gwen's elbows stuck out a bit, and Bridget let her reins get too long in the air. Maybe Seren could have tucked his knees more evenly, and I could have spotted a better distance.

But as far as I was concerned, it was the perfect jump.

APPENDIX

Cymru (Wales)

Wales is part of Great Britain, along with England and Scotland. At times, it has been occupied by the Romans, Saxons, Irish, Normans, and English. Throughout the centuries, the Welsh people have kept their own culture and language.

For generations, the Welsh language was banned in schools, but was kept alive in rural villages and in people's homes. Today only about 20 percent of the people in the country speak fluent Welsh. However, more schools are teaching some classes in Welsh to keep this ancient language alive. The Welsh word for Wales is *Cymru* (pronounced *KUHM-ree*).

When British Prime Minister Neville Chamberlain declared war on Germany in 1939, Welsh and English soldiers fought side by side, along with the rest of the Allied forces. More than two-thirds of Great Britain's food was imported at the time, but the nation had to become more self-reliant during the war. This meant a big increase in the production of grain, meat, vegetables, and milk, as well as new crops like flax to make fabric. Chamberlain's successor, Prime Minister Winston Churchill, famously called Great Britain's farms the "front line of freedom."

In September 1939, 1.5 million children were evacuated from their homes in London and other English cities as part of a government plan called Operation Pied Piper. Children as young as five were sent away to live with host families in the countryside of England and Wales, where, it was believed, German attacks would be less likely. For the first year of the war, no bombs fell, and the war began to seem like a false alarm.

Then, the following September, the Nazi army launched the first air strikes on London, known as the Blitz. The Welsh cities of Cardiff and Swansea were bombed as well. Children who were evacuated had no way of knowing whether their families were safe. For some children, fleeing the war meant leaving the crowded city and seeing the countryside for the first time. Many evacuees developed close relationships with their host families, often staying in contact with them for the rest of their lives.

Germany surrendered to the Allied forces on

May 8, 1945. This came to be known as VE Day, for Victory in Europe. But work on the home front didn't end with the war. Because of the need to provide food relief to other countries, including Germany, rationing grew even stricter. Fuel for cars and tractors was in short supply for years to come, so horses and ponies continued to be an important part of daily life in Wales.

FROM CHARIOT TO COAL MINES

Ponies have run wild in the Welsh hills since before Roman times. Harnesses from the Bronze Age show that ponies less than twelve hands high pulled wagons and war chariots. In medieval Britain, knights' squires rode small ponies called rouncyes, which trotted all day to keep up with destriers (warhorses) that might be nearly twice their size.

In 1540, King Henry VIII ordered that all stallions under fifteen hands and mares under thirteen hands be slaughtered. He thought the cavalry needed bigger, stronger horses to win wars.

Fortunately, some hardy Welsh ponies survived by staying high in the mountains. In modern times, wild herds still run free in the Snowdonia and Brecon Beacons National Parks. It was a happy day for ponies when Henry VIII's daughter, Queen Elizabeth I, took the throne and repealed the Horses Act.

In later centuries, Welsh ponies and cobs were used as coach horses in cities, as draft animals on farms, and as pit ponies in one of Wales's biggest industries, coal mining. The shortest pit ponies were sent into tunnels that ran for many miles underground, often with children who could squeeze into spaces too small for adults. The last pit pony in Great Britain retired in 1999.

THE ABCs OF WELSH PONIES

In 1901, a minister from West Wales named Reverend Owen started the Welsh Pony and Cob Society. His church was always full, but some townsfolk suggested this was not because people came to hear his sermons but because they wanted to admire his beautiful ponies!

Today the Welsh breed registry is split into several groups.

Section A is the Welsh Mountain pony. As the smallest breed members, standing under

twelve hands, Welsh Mountain ponies often have a slightly "wild" look and feisty nature. Perhaps this trait goes back to their ancestors that escaped Henry VIII's sword.

Section B is the Welsh pony, under 13.2 hands. This type was created by crossing Welsh Mountain ponies with Arabian and Thoroughbred lines to create a gentle, pretty riding pony for children. Like Lily, who would be registered in this section, many Welsh ponies are talented jumpers.

Section C is the Welsh pony of cob type, under 13.2 hands. Cobs are sturdy ponies or horses of a slight draft type, with small, attractive heads and long, silky hair, or "feathers," on their legs.

Section D is the Welsh cob, over 13.2 hands. The Welsh cob was often called the ideal family horse. Through the 1900s, many doctors, preachers, and traveling salesmen relied on a sturdy Welsh cob rather than a car to carry them across the rough countryside. Wealthy landowners used them for fox hunting as well.

About the Pony Club

The Institute of the Horse was a club started in England to promote equestrian sports. In 1929, the Pony Club became its official youth division. Pony Club is meant to teach proper horse care, good sportsmanship, and enjoyment of riding.

Pony Club members take tests to earn ratings

as their skills grow. With a few months of lessons, most riders can earn the D rating, or basic certificate. Most Pony Clubbers are able to achieve a C rating, which calls for a higher level of riding, including jumping. It also requires more in-depth knowledge of feeding, grooming, common illnesses, first aid, and the history of horsemanship. B and A ratings are awarded only to advanced riders after years of study.

These days, Pony Club has gone international. The United States Pony Club was founded in 1954. More than thirty countries have at least one branch, and the worldwide membership is over 130,000. Several Olympic gold medalists, including three-day eventer David O'Conner and show jumper Melanie Smith Taylor, are former Pony Club members.

HORSE GAMES

Riders have played games on horseback for centuries. Their original purpose was to prepare for hunting and war. For example, the word *carousel* comes from the Italian *carosello*, meaning "little war." In this game, riders try to throw a spear through brass rings hung from colored ribbons. Some Native American tribes used mounted races and games called *o'mok'see* to teach skills needed to track and kill buffalo.

Today, the United Kingdom and parts of the United States call games on horseback *gymkhana*. This word from India means "ball court." Gymkhana races often take the form of team relays. Classic games include pole bending, stepping stones, egg and spoon, sack races, and flag races.

Other countries with Pony Club chapters take turns hosting international gymkhanas. Visiting teams fly around the world to compete on borrowed horses. The prizes look different depending on where the riders are showing. In Great Britain and Canada, the first-place ribbon is red and second-place is blue. In the United States and Australia, it's the blue ribbon people really want to win!

ABOUT THE AUTHOR

Whitney Sanderson has loved horses since she was a child, riding in a 4-H club and reading series like The Saddle Club and The Black Stallion. In addition to always having a horse or two in the backyard, she grew up surrounded by beautiful equine artwork created by her mother, Horse Diaries illustrator Ruth Sanderson. Whitney is the author of Horse Diaries #5: *Golden Sun* and Horse Diaries #10: *Darcy*, as well as another chapter book called *Horse Rescue: Treasure*.

ABOUT THE ILLUSTRATOR

Ruth Sanderson grew up with a love for horses. She has illustrated and retold many fairy tales and likes to feature horses in them whenever possible. Her book about a magical horse, *The Golden Mare, the Firebird, and the Magic Ring*, won the Texas Bluebonnet Award.

Ruth and her daughter have two horses, an Appaloosa named Thor and a quarter horse named Gabriel. She lives with her family in Massachusetts.

To find out more about her adventures with horses and the research she does to create Horse Diaries illustrations, visit her website, ruthsanderson.com.

⪦ Collect all the books in the ⪧ Horse Diaries series!

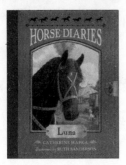

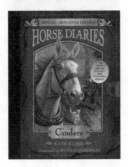